THE
MAGNIFICENT

I

A
LITTLE
ARK
BOOK

ALLEN & UNWIN

D1630846

Paperback edition
First published 1991
A Little Ark Book
Allen & Unwin Pty Ltd
9 Atchison Street, St Leonards,
NSW 2065 Australia

National Library of Australia
Cataloguing-in-Publication entry:

Fienberg, Anna.
The magnificent nose and other marvels.
ISBN 1 86373 110 5.
I. Gamble, Kim. II. Title.
A823.3

Set in Baskerville by Bookset, Melbourne
Printed in Singapore by South Wind
10 9 8 7 6 5 4

CONTENTS

For my sister, Linda, with love. A. F.
For Belinda. K. G.

1
LINDALOU
and her Golden Gift

WHEN LINDALOU was born, her mother and father were surprised.

Her aunt fainted.

The cat's whiskers fell off.

For curled in each of Lindalou's little fists were two strange and beautiful things. In her right hand lay a tiny golden hammer. In her left lay a golden nail.

Lindalou was a quiet baby. She smiled when her mother filled her cradle with teddies and ducks and woolly tigers. But she didn't play with them.

Lindalou played only with her tiny golden hammer and tiny golden nail.

When a year had passed, Lindalou said her first word.

'Wood,' she said, clear as a bell.

'Wood?' said her mother, puzzled. But off she went to the timber yard that lay at the edge of the forest. She chose for her daughter a piece from each and every kind of wood that she found there.

When another year had passed, Linda said her second words.

'More wood,' she said, clear as a bell.

'More wood?' said her mother, puzzled.

'Yes,' said Lindalou. 'I want a piece of rosewood for its purple heart, a piece of sassafras for its tiger stripes, and a piece of satinwood because it is as fine and golden as my little hammer.'

'But what are you going to make?' asked her mother.

'Something,' said Lindalou, and smiled.

Lindalou was no longer a quiet baby. She hammered and sang, and sang and hammered. At the end of the first week she had made a box.

The box was the size of a duck's egg, and just as smooth. Its corners were as rounded as cheeks, and the satinwood glowed and rippled like the sun on water.

'She's really very good,' said her mother, looking closely.

'She's really very loud,' said her father, blocking his ears.

While Lindalou worked, someone was looking over her shoulder. His name was Aristan, and he came from a long line of magic spiders. Swinging there on the wall, he shone like a dab of butter, for he was as golden as Linda's little hammer and nail.

'What will I put in the box?' Linda would ask herself each day.

'Secrets,' Aristan would whisper.

Linda liked making boxes, and she liked having Aristan for company. Soon she was singing and hammering so loudly that her parents could not sleep. Her mother bought a set of earplugs. Her father wore a pillow around his head.

'For mercy's sake, get rid of the golden hammer!' shouted her aunt when she came to visit.

But how could they take away the golden gifts that came into the world with Lindalou?

By the end of the third week, Lindalou had made another two boxes. They were perfect, like the first, but different. One was made from sassafras, for its tiger stripes, and the other from rosewood, for its purple heart.

Lindalou was pleased with her boxes. She lined them up on the floor, next to her bed, so that she could look at them before she fell asleep.

That night, Linda dreamed of a house in the trees. It was shaped like a boat, moored between two branches. Lindalou stood at the window, steering her boat-house into an ocean of sky.

'Now I'll sail past the stars at night and hammer and sing amongst the trees by day,' she said in her dream.

When Lindalou awoke the next morning, she bent down to look at her boxes. She picked the first one up and opened it.

Inside she found tiny golden tools! There was a saw for cutting wood, a clamp for holding wood in place, and a plane to smooth its edges. As she took out each piece, it began to shine and hum and grow until it was just the right size for her hand.

In the second box she found small pieces of wood: the ones she knew, and *new* kinds: ebony and silky oak and cedar. As she took them out, each piece began to shine and hum and grow until the whole room was filled with wood.

In the third box, Lindalou found a piece of paper rolled up and tied with golden threads. Inside was Aristan. He was moving quickly across the page, leaving a trail of fine spidery lines.

When he had finished, and Lindalou saw what he had made, she laughed with joy. There on the page was a plan of the house in her dream!

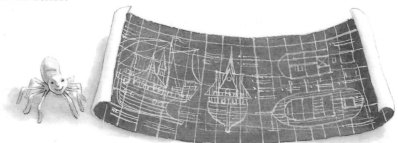

No-one saw Lindalou—or Aristan—for a week. Her parents found a note tacked on her door: *Away on Business.*

The house was very quiet without Lindalou. Her mother took off her earplugs. Her father left his pillow on the bed. Even the cat's whiskers grew back.

'You can hear a pin drop, without Lindalou,' said her mother.

'Who wants to hear a pin drop?' said her father. And off they went to find Lindalou.

Through the forest they walked, searching and calling, until they came to the timber yard.

'Have you seen a little girl pass this way?' they asked the man chopping wood.

'Yes,' he said. 'She was heading for the other side of the forest.'

On they hurried now, along the twisting paths of the forest, calling 'Lindalou! Linda . . . *lou!*' and as they ran, aunts and uncles, cousins and friends came to join them.

They drew near a stream, and a sound of singing and hammering filled the air.

'That's my girl!' cried her father, and they searched the long grasses and between the rocks, but still they couldn't find Lindalou.

Then a shout came down from the tree tops. 'Up here!' called a voice, and there, between the branches of a maple tree, perched the most magnificent house anyone had ever seen. And in the doorway, smiling at them all, was Lindalou.

'Come in!' she called.

So, up the rope stairs went her mother and father. Up climbed her aunt and uncle, her friends and the woodchopper. Last of all came the cat.

'Welcome to my new house,' said Lindalou. 'Here I can hammer and sing by day and sail past the stars at night.' She looked over at Aristan, swinging there on the wall. 'Tonight we are going to Kathmandu. Would anyone like to come?'

'*We* would!' cried her mother and father.

'*I* would!' said the woodchopper.

'How do we get there?' asked her aunt.

'Simple,' replied Lindalou. 'Do you see this steering wheel and the little lever? When I push the lever, the house rises up into the clouds, and this is how I steer.'

'Are there any tigers in Kathmandu?' asked the woodchopper nervously. But only the cat was listening.

Everyone hurried home to fetch their pyjamas and tooth-brushes, and Lindalou opened her *Guide to Kathmandu*.

That evening, as the sun was setting, the birds of the forest saw a strange sight. A beautiful wooden house rose above the treetops and went sailing past. It was filled with smiling people and a startled cat, all waving from the windows, and a ripple of happy voices drifted back as the house became a tiny speck in the distance.

2
ANDY UMM
and the Silliaza Circus

ANDY UMM was small and pale and weedy. He was the kind of boy people ordered about, or forgot.

When his mother sent him to the shops, he was always the last person to be served. His father would go to fetch him and, on the way home, explain to him how he should Stand Up For Himself. Andy Umm always listened politely.

He was used to listening, for everyone had something to say about Andy.

'He's as quiet as a mouse,' said his aunt.

'He's as close as a clam,' said his uncle.

'He wouldn't say boozlebom to a goose,' said his sister.

But nobody knew what went on inside Andy Umm. Nobody knew what he was listening to when he sat so quietly at the window each day.

When the time came for him to go out and make his own way in the world, his mother sighed and gave him a last dose of her special Growing Medicine.

'Speak up, now,' she told him. 'Mind you step out boldly.'

'And remember, Stand Up For Yourself,' his father added.

Andy did step out boldly, but, not being quite sure of his way in the world, he wandered for many days. He passed through towns where lights burned like eyes in the windows. He crept through forests as dark as caves.

And with each day he grew more hungry and afraid.

At the end of one weary day, Andy came to a large clearing. There, perched on a hill was a group of coloured tents. He crept closer and saw ladies in shiny tights, and a man walking like a bird on a wire. He saw horses with red ribbons, dogs, an elephant, and a cage full of lions! Andy sniffed the busy smell of animals, and smiled. *What do u think andy can see?*

He headed for the big orange tent. From the flag pole, a sky-blue sign waved in the breeze: 'SILLIAZA CIRCUS', it announced. 'WORLD FAMOUS ACROBATS, LION TAMERS, ARISTAN'S DANCING FLEAS!' And underneath, in only slightly smaller letters, 'MR SILLIAZA — MANAGER'.

Now it happened that Mr Silliaza was in need of a Cleaner and Animal Feeder.

For the first time, Andy did what his mother had told him. He spoke up. 'I'm the man for the job!' he said.

Mr Silliaza stared at Andy. 'Well,' he said slowly, 'maybe,' but he shook his head at Andy's skinny arms and shy ways. 'Mind the elephant doesn't step on you!' he said, and laughed.

For Mr Silliaza didn't know what went on inside Andy Umm.

But Bertha the elephant did. So did Basil the chimp. And Nathan the horse. And all the show dogs and the dancing fleas. They had never had a Cleaner and Animal Feeder like Andy.

For Andy could speak their language. *What do u think is diff with Andy?*

'Hello,' said Andy to Bertha in perfect Elephant talk. 'Would you fancy a nice barrel of bamboo?'

'Hi there,' he greeted Basil in excellent Chimp, 'would you care for a Banana Whip?'

Now Andy loved to talk—with the animals, that is. He had an opinion on everything, and the animals liked to ask his advice. Nathan consulted him about his teeth (they ached), and Basil told him about his dreams (they were scary). Late at night, Andy sat up with Bertha and they swayed to her favourite records.

The only animal that Andy didn't talk to was Fidel the Ferocious. Fidel was the fiercest lion in the circus. When he roared the tents shook and the dogs howled. Sir Leonard Lately, World Famous Lion Tamer, was the only man who could handle him in the ring. Sir Leonard was a cruel man who waved a whip about as if it were a handkerchief. He made Fidel jump through a hoop of fire. Often, after a show, Fidel would return to his cage smarting and sore from Sir Leonard's wicked whip. Fidel growled when anyone came near, and all the animals kept out of his way.

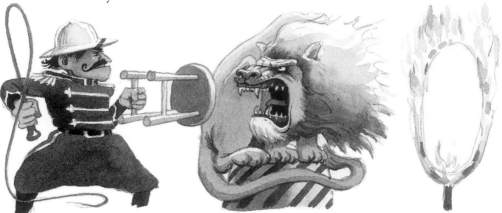

Now, Andy's special friend was Aristan, the ringmaster of the Flea Circus. He was a spider who had seen much of the world, and he could always answer Andy's questions.

'Why is Fidel so ferocious?' Andy asked. 'He never lets anyone near him.'

'He is sad because Daphne has disappeared,' said Aristan.

'Daphne?'

'Yes. Everyone loved Daphne, but she was Fidel's particular friend. She was a very special mouse, you see. She used to tell him stories about the jungle, and when his ears were ringing from the cracking of Sir Leonard's whip she would sing him to sleep with gentle lullabies.'

'Fidel likes *lullabies*?' Andy was surprised. 'When did Daphne go?'

'She left shortly before you joined the circus, and now Fidel gets crosser every day.'

After this talk with Aristan, Andy tried to get close to Fidel. He crept up to the cage and looked into Fidel's golden eyes. But Fidel would only growl, and then roar, until Mr Silliaza bustled over and pushed him away.

Andy liked the circus, and talking with the animals, but the sadness of Fidel lay heavy within him now as if it were his own.

Then, on the morning of the Grand Opening at Fez, the circus was awakened by Mr Silliaza.

'Help! Disaster! Ruin and Doom!' he cried as he ran between the tents, clutching his dressing gown to his chest. The High-wire Walkers, the Clowns and the Jugglers came stumbling out, their eyes still closed with sleep.

'Sir Leonard has packed his bags and gone!' shrieked Mr Silliaza.

'Why?' cried a juggler.

'He says Fidel is too ferocious. "I won't work any longer with that bad-tempered beast." Those were his very words!' Mr Silliaza wrung his hands. 'Our best act is ruined. Who else could ever handle Fidel the Ferocious? No, it's going to be Lion Stew for dinner tonight. I'm through with that mangy animal!'

A small voice came from the back of the crowd.

'Er, I think I could handle him, Sir,' said Andy. There was a snort from the crowd, then giggles, then a great wave of laughter that made Andy cover his pink face with shame.

At last Mr Silliaza said, 'Well, we're ruined anyway. Why don't we try it? Andy and Fidel—what a show that would be, if he doesn't eat you alive, my boy!'

15

Afterwards, Andy sat alone in the tent and trembled.

At that moment, Aristan arrived on Andy's shoulder.

'Daphne is your only hope, I'm afraid,' he said.

'But how can I find her?' cried Andy.

'Ask the fieldmice who live at the edge of the wheat field,' Aristan replied. 'They are Daphne's cousins, and may know where she's gone.'

The air trembled with another bad-tempered roar.

'Hurry,' said Aristan.

And so Andy fetched his jacket and set out to search for Daphne. As he hurried toward the field he called in perfect Mouse, 'Excuse me, is anyone there? I'd like to give a message to your cousin Daphne. Hello? Hello?'

After a moment a voice near Andy's boots squeaked, 'Mind your feet! Who are you?'

Andy bent down and chatted for some time with the mouse (who went by the name of Denton) and discovered that Daphne

was now living near the bank of the river that bordered the next field.

Andy walked for a long time amongst the reeds and the hanging willows by the river, calling, 'Daphne! Daphneee!' His socks were soaked and his legs grew cold as the shadows deepened across the water.

Andy sat down beside a large willow and put his head in his hands. Just then he felt something run up his leg.

'I believe you're looking for me,' said the bright-whiskered mouse on his knee. 'My name is Daphne.'

who do u think its going to be

'Oh, I'm so pleased to meet you!' exclaimed Andy, and he began to tell her about Fidel and the sadness and the terrible ferocity.

As Daphne listened, her eyes grew narrow and she hissed at the mention of the lion tamer's name. Her whiskers quivered when Andy spoke of the lion stew. 'I'll come with you at once,' she said, 'but first I must call my children.'

'Children?' gasped Andy.

'Yes!' replied Daphne. 'That was why I went away. I didn't want my babies to be born in the circus, where the likes of Sir Leonard or that Silliaza are always setting traps for us. Those men aren't fond of mice, you know. But for Fidel I'll come back, and then we'll see.' And she scooted down the hole in the willow tree to fetch her babies.

Now Andy filled his pockets with Daphne and her six babies, and headed back across the field. The mice wriggled and tickled and bumped as he trudged over the rough ground to the circus, but they were thrilled as he told them about his plan for the next performance.

That night, the circus blazed with lights. It floated in the dark like a warm, glowing planet. Andy hid in the shadows at the side of the big tent. He swallowed nervously and peeked at all the people lined up to see him. Daphne and her babies were already in position, hidden under a seat near the exit.

Now Andy stumbled into the ring. He was wearing Sir Leonard's large trousers, and he tripped over the cuffs.

'Er, good evening all,' he said, 'Tonight you will see a most interesting, that is, er, a Spectacular Event. I would like to introduce the King of the Jungle—Fidel the Ferocious!'

Andy stepped into the cage and snapped his fingers.

Out padded Fidel. He lifted his great head and gave a roar that crashed through the air like thunder.

'Bring on the Circles of Fire!' cried Andy, and the Clowns bounded into the ring, wheeling five enormous hoops. The audience gasped as a Clown put his torch to them and they flamed into a long tunnel of fire.

'Now, er, Fidel, I'd like you to jump carefully through these rather dangerous hoops,' said Andy. 'That is, if you would like to, of course,' he added politely.

'*Five* hoops of fire?' whispered Mr Silliaza. 'Is he mad? And where's his whip? Stupid boy, he'll be eaten alive!'

Fidel glared at Andy. He shook his mane and growled deep in his belly. Mothers grabbed their children and their purses, ready to run.

'Fidel, look!' Andy spoke firmly. 'Look who's there!' And he pointed to Daphne and her children, waiting just beyond the last hoop.

Fidel peered through the hoops of fire. He saw Daphne hopping up and down, waving and calling, 'Come on Fidel! Come and see my babies!'

Now Fidel bounded into the air. In one glorious leap he sailed through the first hoop, landing neatly on his front paws. He sprang again through the second and third hoops, and was so full of happiness and delight that he somersaulted like an acrobat after the fourth. Up and over, over and up he jumped, until he was soaring like a swift golden arrow through the last and coming to rest at the side of his dear, familiar Daphne.

Everywhere, people jumped up from their seats, clapping and shouting, 'Bravo! Stupendous! What a show!' But Andy was watching Fidel, quiet now, as Daphne and her babies clambered over his paws and told him the grand story of how Andy had found them and brought them back to the circus.

At last the cheering and clapping faded, and Mr Silliaza skipped out into the ring. In his hands was a bunch of roses, and on his face an enormous grin.

'This will be something to tell your grandchildren!' he told the audience. 'About the courage of a young boy—and the taming of a lion!'

He thrust the roses into Andy's hands. 'Will you stay on, Andy, as our new Head Lion Tamer?'

Fidel padded over to Andy and growled into his ear, 'The best Lion Tamer in the history of the world.'

And so, if you visit the circus today, you will see that the sky-blue sign is waving a new message: 'SILLIAZA CIRCUS, WITH ANDROCLES AND THE LION — WORLD'S BRAVEST ANIMAL ACT'.

'I always told him to stand up for himself,' Andy's father remembers proudly.

20

3
CURIOUS FERDINAND
and his
Magic Spectacles

FERDINAND FEEDELBENZ was a boy people noticed. It wasn't that he was noisy. He liked to listen rather than speak. He preferred to ask questions rather than answer them. What was remarkable about Ferdinand Feedelbenz was his curiosity. For Ferdinand wanted to know everything.

'Why does Aunt Ezra always wear gloves?' he would ask his parents when they went to visit.

'Ssh!' said his father, out of the corner of his mouth.

'Quiet!' said his mother, rattling her tea cup.

But Ferdinand liked to ask questions.

'Why does Uncle Fez have hair growing out of his nose?' he would ask, his eyes fixed on his uncle's fuzz.

'Curiosity killed the cat,' his father hissed.

'No,' said Ferdinand, thinking this over. 'Curiosity leads to Greatness.'

Ferdinand was curious about most things, but particularly about the human body. He was thrilled by Warts. He was fascinated by Lumps. And he was drawn, like a bee to honey, by the miracle of Moles.

Books on the human body lined his walls, and were stacked in wobbly piles on his desk. He had 1,423 medical magazines, and a subscription to *The Up-To-Date Doctor*.

Ferdinand often wandered the markets, hoping to add to his collection. There, he could stroll amongst the stalls of candied fruit and antique brooches, and sort through the cheap books for one of his favourite kind.

And it was at the markets, one extraordinary Sunday, that his curiosity led to Greatness.

Ferdinand was looking through a box of old books when he came across the pair of spectacles. They were ancient, with wire frames, and when he put them on the world blushed slightly pink, as if all its veins were showing. 'Now here is a curious thing,' murmured Ferdinand.

'Have them,' said the man at the stall. 'Those specs are as old as I am. No-one else would want them.'

Ferdinand loved his new spectacles. He wandered amongst the stalls, trying to catch a glimpse of himself in the mirrors. He was staring at his reflection when a little girl crashed into the pickled herring stall, and fell off her bike.

Wailing with pain, she held out her arm. Ferdinand peered down. He took off his spectacles. He polished them with his hanky. He put them on again.

'Truly amazing,' he whispered, and then to the people gathering around he said, 'This child has a clean break of the radius—the shorter bone, that is, of the forearm.'

And sure enough, when the girl and her mother went to the hospital, that is what the X-rays showed.

Ferdinand didn't tell anyone about his spectacles. Their magic was his secret power. With his glasses he could see right through skin and flesh to the dark, pumping world below.

Ferdinand no longer preferred to ask questions. Now he liked to answer them.

'Aunt Ezra,' Ferdinand said when his aunt complained of itchy spots on her hands, 'I believe you have a bad case of Imbezelia. If you will just use this ointment, twice a day, you can throw away your gloves forever.'

Aunt Ezra was delighted.

Mr and Mrs Feedelbenz were astounded.

Ferdinand polished his glasses fondly.

'Uncle Fez, I believe you have an inflamed appendix,' Ferdinand said when his uncle complained of tummy ache. 'I suggest you go to the hospital without delay.'

And Uncle Fez had his appendix out that afternoon.

Ferdinand's fame began to spread. He could diagnose rare tropical diseases and galloping fevers in just sixty seconds. Sometimes the Specialists and Brain Surgeons agreed with him, and sometimes they didn't. But Ferdinand was always right.

Now Mrs Feedelbenz had to keep an appointment book, because so many people wanted to see Ferdinand. She bought him a stethoscope, a little black bag, and a crisp white coat. All his patients agreed that he had an excellent bedside manner.

With the knowledge of 1,423 medical magazines up his sleeve, Ferdinand always knew what to prescribe once he had discovered the Disease. Soon he was asked to give Lectures, and hold Conferences in exotic parts of the world. Ferdinand was pleased about this, because he was curious to see how other people lived.

One day, the Prime Minister of the land sent for him. He was suffering from a disease that made his inner ear tickle, and his brain itch. Not one of the doctors he had seen could discover what was the matter with him. The Prime Minister was becoming desperate. He couldn't concentrate on making new laws and public holidays, and his wife was fed up with saying everything twice.

When Ferdinand heard the news, he was very excited. He put on his crisp white coat, picked up his black bag, and felt in his pocket for his spectacles. But his pocket was empty.

Ferdinand panicked.

Had he left them on the desk? The mantelpiece? Under the pillow? Had the cat eaten them?

'Come on, Ferdinand, you'll be late,' said his mother, jangling her keys.

And so off went Ferdinand—without his secret power—to see the most important man in the land.

The Prime Minister was a big, hairy man who shaved three times a day. In spite of all this shaving, the hair above his lip and in his ears was as bushy as a State Forest.

'That's the boy, have a look in my ear,' he boomed at Ferdinand.

There was nothing for it but to climb up on the Prime Minister's knee, and peer into his ear. What Ferdinand saw was more hair, and a normal, dried-apricot kind of ear.

'Hmm,' he said, uncertainly, playing for time.

'What do you see there, boy?' said the Prime Minister.

Ferdinand swallowed.

'Speak up, Ferdinand,' his mother urged.

'Cat got your tongue?' the Prime Minister barked.

All the Ministers, and Secretaries of State, and Brain Surgeons cleared their throats and tapped their fingers impatiently on the desk.

Ferdinand brought out his stethoscope and listened to the Prime Minister's chest. Then he opened his little black bag and pulled out his auriscope, for looking inside ears.

Nothing.

Ferdinand took a deep breath. 'Well, I'm afraid I can't—'

The door opened and Mr Feedelbenz burst in. 'Sorry to interrupt,' he bowed. 'Oh Ferdinand, I have your spectacles here. Took them to work instead of mine this morning. Have you found the trouble yet?'

Ferdinand nearly fainted with joy, and finished his sentence. '—see without my spectacles.'

When Ferdinand put on his magic spectacles, he could see the whole, complete, inner workings of the Prime Minister's brain. He also saw a long golden thread, as fine as a spiderweb. Did it lead somewhere? Was something *spinning* that thread?

'Er,' said Ferdinand. 'Have you ever considered the possibility that something is *alive* in there?'

There was a shocked silence. Then the Prime Minister guffawed. The Ministers giggled. The Brain Surgeons slapped their knees.

'Never mind, Dear,' said Mrs Feedelbenz, patting her son's hand.

But Ferdinand looked again.

'Just as I thought,' he said. And from his little black bag he took a pair of pincers.

'This might tickle,' he warned the Prime Minister. Then delicately, slowly, he set to work.

For sixty long seconds Ferdinand pulled and pulled and pulled at the fine gold thread. He pulled until out popped a small golden spider.

'Well, dash all dunderheads!' roared the Prime Minister. 'So that's what it was!'

Aristan (for that was the spider's name) waved his legs at Ferdinand as he swung back and forth on his long golden thread.

'I've heard of this spider,' said Ferdinand.

Now all the Ministers and Secretaries of State cheered for Ferdinand. 'True genius,' they cried.

'Who'd have thought it?' the Brain Surgeons whispered.

'This boy will be our first International Expert for All Human Diseases!' the Prime Minister declared.

'It was nothing,' said Ferdinand modestly, looking down at Aristan. 'May I keep this spider?'

'Certainly, dear boy, certainly,' the Prime Minister replied, 'and is there anything else that takes your fancy?'

'A new Dictionary of Diseases would be nice,' said Ferdinand, as the First Secretary showed him out. 'With an index,' he added as they shut the door.

And that is the true story of how the curiosity of Ferdinand Feedelbenz led to Greatness.

4
IGNATIUS BINZ
and his
Magnificent Nose

NOW, THERE are two things you should know about Ignatius Binz: one is that he was born on top of a perfume factory, and the other is that he had a magnificent nose.

Not that his nose was particularly pretty, being small and freckled and snubbed, much like any other nose. It was what this nose could *do* that was extraordinary.

Ignatius had not been in the world for very long before his mother noticed something unusual; her son smiled when she made spicy sauces. He spat out his dummy and his nose sniffed happily as the fragrance of rich foods drifted up. By the time he could crawl, Ignatius could tell you in one sniff exactly what was cooking for dinner. And on his mother's birthday he created a new sauce so delicious that tears came to the family's eyes.

'The boy has inherited his grandfather's nose!' Mrs Binz cried. 'With him in the business, our factory will be great again. Everyone will want perfume by Binz.'

Mrs Binz didn't believe in wasting time. As soon as Ignatius could walk, she took him on a tour of the Binz Perfume Factory. He liked putting his nose into the little test-tubes, all neatly labelled and smelling of spice and blossom. But most interesting were those bottles of woody, crisp smells that came from mosses and ferns. There were little pictures on these bottles, of forests with rain-shiny leaves, and trees that grew as high as you could see. Ignatius would have liked to visit these places, but his father told him not to be silly.

'Perfume, my boy, that's your calling. Why bother to *go* to a place when you can smell it in a bottle? Ignatius Binz, the world is at the end of your nose.'

Ignatius looked down at the floor of the perfume factory and thought the world must be a rather flat kind of place, but he didn't say anything more about travelling.

As Ignatius grew, so did the remarkable powers of his nose. Blindfolded, he could tell you the name of any scent. In a finger-snap he could make a fragrance of his own. Now Ignatius spent all his time downstairs at the factory. He wore a white coat and sat in a clean windowless office. Stacked on shelves around him were bottles of chemicals starting with B, and books about the History of Perfume. But all Ignatius really needed was his nose.

His nose told him many things: which smells were the most delicious, and how much more delicious they would be if he added, say, just a hint of wood pine.

Now Ignatius was inventing perfumes no-one had ever imagined. His perfumes made people dream of impossible things: flowers in the snow, starlight at noon, desert roses. His perfumes shocked, startled, *sang*. Mr Binz called them 'Desert Ice' and 'Moroccan Moon', and they sold very well.

But alone in his room at night, Ignatius wondered if there mightn't be more to life than perfume. It wasn't very exciting, he thought, to sit in an office with a lot of test tubes. And was it, Ignatius wondered deep in his soul, very useful?

Ignatius longed for Adventure, Travel and Danger. He saw himself saving lives, rescuing people from explosions and certain death. He wanted to see the world!

But his mother only patted his head. 'Your fortune, Ignatius Binz, is in your nose. And you don't have to go far to find that!'

One day, as Ignatius bent over a fresh tub of gardenias, he saw something moving under the petals. Reaching in, he lifted the creature up on his finger. A tiny golden spider, no bigger than a bud, crawled into his palm and waved at him.

'Hello,' said Ignatius.

'How do you do?' said the spider.

From that moment, Ignatius was best friends with Aristan. (Yes, that was the spider's name.) While Ignatius mixed rose and jasmine petals and sniffed his test-tubes, Aristan kept him company. Swinging gently from a strand of his web, he told Ignatius about the world beyond the factory—about forests with rain-shiny leaves and trees that grow as high as you can see.

'I would like to visit those places,' Ignatius said.

'You can!' replied Aristan. 'Your nose is very special, but it is made for more than perfumes. Saving lives could be your destiny! Just think, you could smell danger before anyone. Find it and remember it—the smell of danger.'

With Aristan's words in his ear, and a suitcase in his hand, Ignatius set off to see the world. He walked through jungles steaming in the sun. He smelled fresh cut grass and the salt of the ocean. Sometimes, he camped under trees that grew as high as he could see. 'Having a lovely time,' he wrote to his parents, as he ate marshmallows in the moonlight.

One afternoon, when he'd reached the outskirts of a city, a strange smell tickled his nose. It was sharp, peppery, smouldering. 'Aha!' thought Ignatius, 'at last! *This* is the smell of danger.'

He sniffed. His nose told him the burning was far away, but the smell hung like an echo on the air, pulling him toward it.

Now he began to run, and as he ran night fell, furring the streets with darkness. Deeper and deeper into the city he ran, following his nose through winding alleys and around shadowy corners until the smell of burning became so strong that he knew he had arrived.

'BOTTLED GAS FACTORY', the sign said on the building in front of him. And in smaller letters, 'Danger—keep out'.

Ignatius shivered. He knew about gas and fire from working at the perfume factory. If a flame just breathed on those bottles of gas, an explosion like a volcano would erupt.

He crept round the outside of the building and peered into the windows. The great, dark rooms were full of pipes and machinery. There was no-one about; just the dark and the smell of danger. And then he saw it.

In a small room at the back of the factory a pile of rags lay smouldering. Even as he watched, a spark kindled, and a red glow, as fierce as sunset, lit up the room. It showed him books and files and boxes of paper, and flames now danced angrily between them. He gasped as the flames joined and swelled until they almost reached the ceiling. At any moment the whole factory could go up.

Ignatius hurtled back down the path—up the hill, along the street, past the darkened doorways. He found a phone box and dialled Emergency.

'The Fire Brigade, please, to the Bottled Gas Factory,' he said. 'And step on it!'

When the big red fire engines came roaring down the street, Ignatius was ready for them.

'Follow me!' he cried, and ten, twenty, thirty men—in blue uniforms with shiny buttons—leaped out and ran after him.

Ignatius led them around to the room at the back, just in time to see the flames shatter the glass of its windows. He watched as the men shouted orders to each other, hauling out hoses as fat as pythons.

'Water on!' they shouted, and, 'Ten metres to the left!'

Ignatius thought his heart would burst with pride as the jets of water shot over the flames.

The next day, back at the perfume factory, Mr and Mrs Binz were having their breakfast. Mr Binz gave a start of surprise when he spotted his son on the front page of the newspaper.

'Small boy saves city,' he read aloud to his wife.

'Hmm?' she said, sipping her tea.

'The magnificent nose of Ignatius Binz led him to a fire,' read on Mr Binz, 'that could have destroyed the city of Springstep. The Mayor of Springstep said yesterday, "Ignatius Binz is the kind of man we need in this town."'

'Fancy that!' said Mr Binz, putting down the paper.

'He was born with his grandfather's nose,' said Mrs Binz fondly.

That day, Mr and Mrs Binz went to Springstep. They found their son at the top of a tall tower, overlooking the Springstep Forest. With him was a band of men in blue uniforms and shiny buttons, enjoying their lunch and the splendid view.

After the Binzs had met everyone (and eaten lasagne with spicy sauce), Ignatius took them through to his office. 'IGNATIUS BINZ', the sign said on the door, 'CAPTAIN, FIRE BRIGADE'.

Ignatius showed them a desk with nine telephones and a map of the world on the wall. 'I get to travel a lot,' Ignatius told his parents, after they had hugged and kissed and congratulated him. 'Way up here on the tower I can sniff out trouble before it gets started. I deal in fires, floods and any number of Natural Disasters.'

Now Mr and Mrs Binz often left the perfume factory to visit their son, but they didn't always find him at home. For the magnificent nose of Ignatius Binz led him to many different parts of the world: wherever the smell of danger called him.

5
VALENTINA LOOKWELL
and her
Surprising Portraits

VALENTINA LOOKWELL lived in Grimbald Street.
Homer the postman lived next door. *letter*

And next door to *him* lived Fang the bulldog. Not many people were fond of Fang. He had a pushed-in face, as if he'd been in a fight, and a growl like grinding gravel. Homer always tiptoed past his house when delivering the mail, but Fang could hear a snowflake falling. Fang's terrible bark made Homer wish he'd taken his mother's advice, and become a plumber instead of a postman.

But Valentina knew that Fang was not a biter at heart. Just as she knew that Homer was as bold as a bear inside. Ever since she was born, Valentina had been able to look right into people, and see them as they really were.

It wasn't that she tried hard, or stared deep into people's eyes. She was just able to see into people's hearts as easily as looking at a mirror. It was a sort of magic habit of hers.

Now Valentina had another gift as well: she could paint. She painted the flowers and trees and houses of Grimbald Street, and so well did she do it that all the neighbours begged for a picture of their own home.

Valentina liked to paint, but she felt there was something missing in her pictures. She longed to paint something unexpected—a tiger behind a hedge, a goblin on a fence. She wished a neighbour, just once, would ask for a surprise painting.

One day, when Valentina was finishing a drawing of a garden, she glimpsed something moving on her painting. She looked closer and saw, deep inside the heart of a rose, a tiny golden speck. As she stared, the speck grew a head and legs, and stepped off the painting and into her hand.

'Your paintings are very lifelike,' said Aristan (for that was his name).

'I know,' said Valentina, and sighed.

Aristan looked at her more closely. 'I can see that you would like to paint a different kind of picture,' he said. 'Why not use your other gift? You can see people as they really are—paint them so they can see it too. *That* would make a change in the world.'

Valentina listened to Aristan with excitement. She thought about the people she knew—Homer next door and Fang the bulldog. Now *they* would be fun to paint.

Valentina began with Fang. She set up her easel in Homer's backyard and studied Fang through the fence. She itched to paint those pointy teeth and that scowling face. But as she looked she saw Fang how he really was. She saw a cuddly dog with a heart as soft as custard, curled into a lap like a nut in its shell.

'He shouldn't be called Fang,' she cried. 'His real name is Bud!'

And that was the dog she drew.

When she had finished her painting, she pinned it up on Bud's fence.

Now she asked Homer to sit for his portrait. He blushed and squirmed and shifted on his chair. But as she looked she saw Homer as he really was. She saw a wild-west postie, riding a horse over dangerous land. He had spurs at his heels and a mailbag on his shoulder.

And that was the Homer she drew.

When she finished her painting, she tacked it up on Homer's wall.

By the next week, everyone in Grimbald Street noticed the change. They whistled to Bud. They raised their hats to Homer.

For Bud was no longer a growler. And Homer was as brave as a bear.

'How's old Bud today?' Homer boomed, his mailbag swung jauntily over one shoulder. As he strode along he whistled and stroked his new sideburns. He told Mrs Lookwell that he had taken up horse riding. Soon he would be good enough to enter the Grimbald Cup for Bareback Riding.

'He's a different Homer!' Mrs Lookwell exclaimed, after he'd gone.

'It's as if he were under a magic spell,' said Mr Wishbone from No. 4.

'He's just being himself,' Valentina told them, and she smiled.

Now everyone in Grimbald Street wanted a portrait. And Valentina loved painting surprises. She found the poet in Mr Wishbone's heart; she painted the singer Mrs Sitwither had always wanted to be. After she had painted their portraits, people began to admit their secret wishes. They took dancing lessons, entered baking contests and went camping in wild and dangerous places. Grimbald Street blossomed with cheerfully painted houses, and there were parties and concerts. Mr Wishbone wrote a play; and all day long Mrs Sitwither sang country and western songs as loud as thunder.

Grimbald Street was the happiest and liveliest street in the land, and anyone who came to visit said so.

The only person who wasn't happy or lively was Sir Grimbald. He lived at the end of the street in a grand mansion with twenty-one bedrooms and gold-plated telephones. His gardens were studded with statues but he never wandered amongst them. He was too busy opening bank accounts and plotting new schemes.

Sir Grimbald bought up land like some people collect stamps. He owned every house in Grimbald Street, the park and the pavements and the pebbles in the road. No-one in the street liked Sir Grimbald as he never remembered their names but always told them that the rent was due.

It was Homer who discovered Sir Grimbald's newest and most wicked scheme. One morning, Homer was delivering the mail when a letter fell out of its envelope. He picked it up and saw the name of Sir Grimbald—followed by the fateful words: 'GRIMBALD STREET—SALE'.

The Lookwell family were the first to hear the news.

'Sir Grimbald is selling the street,' announced Homer. 'He's turning it into a Crocodile Park!'

'Fancy a crocodile swimming in my kitchen!' cried Mrs Lookwell. 'The very idea!'

'But I was born in this house! And my mother before me!' exclaimed Mr Lookwell.

'He can't *do* that!' said Valentina.

Well, as it happened, he could. The next day there was a notice about it in the paper. 'CROCODILE PARK FOR GRIMBALD STREET' it said, and everyone was given a month's notice to leave.

Now the street was sad and silent. Mrs Sitwither no longer played the guitar. Mr Wishbone stopped work on his play. And no-one bothered to pat lonely Bud on his pushed-in forehead.

But Homer had not grown bold for nothing. Were they all just going to creep away like mice? he asked. He called a meeting, and this is what he said: 'Now we've never liked Sir Grimbald —' he began.

'He blows cigar smoke in my face!' interrupted Mrs Sitwither.

'—but perhaps he's not wicked all the way through,' Homer went on. 'If Valentina painted his portrait—the way she did mine, you know, how he really is—she might find something else in his character.'

'Like a crocodile!' called out Mr Wishbone.

But everyone agreed that Valentina should try.

It was not easy to paint the portrait of a man like Sir Grimbald. Valentina had to sneak into his garden at night with a torch and her pad and pencils. She peered through the window and studied Sir Grimbald. In the light of his diamond desk light, he was bent over his accounts with a gleeful smile.

Valentina looked and looked, but she could find nothing but bank notes in Sir Grimbald's heart.

Then one night she had an idea. What kind of man, she wondered, had the the *young* Grimbald been?

Now she could see him, fresh from school and bristling with hope. The young Grimbald had wavy hair and romantic eyes, and he once starred as a melancholy knight in a play. He didn't smoke cigars or collect crocodiles back then. He liked theatres, and falling in love.

And that was the Grimbald she drew.

Homer was watching from the footpath when Sir Grimbald discovered the painting. He stared at his younger self, tacked up on the garden wall, and turned crimson with rage.

'What rubbish is this?' he roared, and before he could look any further he tore the painting to pieces.

'What did I tell you?' said Mr Wishbone.

'I'm going to pack,' said Mrs Sitwither, and no-one stopped her.

Soon, men with tape-measures and clipboards began to arrive.

'We'll put a crocodile pool here,' one said, pointing to the Lookwell house.

'And we'll sell crocodile handbags there,' whispered another, pointing to the Wishbone home.

The snapping of jaws could be heard in the distance, and now everyone began to pack.

Everyone except Aristan. He told Valentina and Homer to collect all the pieces of Sir Grimbald's portrait. That night, when Sir Grimbald was sleeping, Aristan worked on the painting. With his fine thread he bound one piece to another until all the parts were held together in the silky web of his magic.

Now Valentina slid open Sir Grimbald's window. Homer crept into his bedroom, and hung the portrait on the wall above his head. There it shone down on the sleeping landlord.

A few days later, Mrs Sitwither was saying goodbye to her friends when Sir Grimbald's limousine came cruising down the street.

'Good morning, Mrs Sitwither!' he cried, leaping out. 'Mr Wishbone, Mr and Mrs Lookwell, how are you? How's the mail business, Homer?'

No-one replied, but Valentina saw a romantic look in Sir Grimbald's eyes, and she smiled.

'How's that play of yours going, Wishbone?' Sir Grimbald burst out. 'Got a producer yet? How about me? I've just bought a theatre where we can put it on.'

'What about the crocodiles?' asked Valentina.

'Crocodiles shmocodiles!' said Sir Grimbald disdainfully. 'Theatre, that's where the money is. Packed houses and the ring of the cash register. And there's fun to be had, life to be lived! Who wants to come to the opera with me?'

And so it happened that Valentina Lookwell made a change in the world, and grew famous for her surprising portraits. And Grimbald Street was once again a happy and lively place, where, thanks to a little magic, there was never a crocodile to be seen, anywhere.

45

6
The Last Word

ONE DAY, a few years later, a boy with a pair of magic spectacles boarded a plane for Kathmandu. He put his luggage on the rack overhead, and sat down next to a boy with a magnificent nose.

The boy with the nose began to sniff. He sniffed so loudly and with such interest that the boy with the spectacles peered at him and said, 'If I'm not mistaken, I would say you have a rare case of Magnificent Nose. I am Ferdinand Feedelbenz, how do you do?'

'I'm Ignatius Binz, of Springstep Fire Brigade, how do you do?'

The two boys found they had much in common, and the conversation turned to travel. They had both been to Peru (where there had recently *nearly* been a huge fire) and they were discussing this when Ignatius felt a tap on his shoulder.

'Excuse me,' said a timid voice from the seat behind, 'but I have never been to Kathmandu. Is it a very fierce kind of place? Oh, my name is Andy, from the Silliaza Circus. How do you do?'

Ignatius showed Andy his guide book, where there was not one fierce photo to be seen, and then the three boys fell to talking.

A little while later, Andy felt a tap on *his* shoulder.

'I couldn't help overhearing,' said the girl in the seat behind him, 'but I'm also going to Kathmandu, and I want to visit a carpenter called Lindalou. If you could just show me your guide book, I might find her house marked on it. Oh, my name is Valentina, how do you do?'

On the map they found a spot marked 'Lindalou's Wooden Treasure'. It said that at her shop you could buy anything you wished—as long as it was made of wood. Lindalou specialised in puppets, tigers, palaces and any-shape-or-size boxes.

'I want a frame,' said Valentina, 'for a painting I'm doing. I like to paint, you see.'

'I like to tame lions,' said Andy shyly.

'Well, I like writing stories,' said an unexpected voice behind them, 'and you all seem like interesting subjects to me.'

'We do?' said Andy.

'Allow me to introduce myself. I'm Wendelin B. Wordforce and I'm on my way to see Lindalou myself. I was going to write her life story, but now I've got a good mind to write a story about the lot of you.'

And so it happened that Valentina, Andy, Ferdinand, Ignatius and Wendelin B. Wordforce all went to see Lindalou. She had another guest staying with her, somebody they all knew.

'Look, it's Aristan!' they cried, and he glowed there on the wall like sunshine. The children had such a wonderful time, they stayed for dinner and then for a year.

Ignatius showed them how to cook spicy sauces, and they all had a go of Ferdinand's spectacles. They went to Andy's new circus (for free!) and at night they would loll on Lindalou's sofa and play cards.

While they played, Wendelin watched and took notes, as writers do. She listened to all their life stories, and the adventures of Aristan, the magic spider. And when a year had passed, and she had finished all her stories, she wrote the last words— the ones you are reading now:

The End